RECEIVED
SEP 24 2011

#10

ON the CASE with
HOLMES and WATSON

SHERLOCK HOLMES

and the Boscombe Valley Mystery

Based on the stories of
Sir Arthur Conan Doyle

Adapted by **Murray Shaw** and **M. J. Cosson**
Illustrated by **Sophie Rohrbach** and **JT Morrow**

GRAPHIC UNIVERSE™ · MINNEAPOLIS · NEW YORK

Grateful acknowledgment to Dame Jean Conan Doyle for permission to use the
Sherlock Holmes characters created by Sir Arthur Conan Doyle

Graphic Universe™
A division of Lerner Publishing Group, Inc.
241 First Avenue North
Minneapolis, MN 55401 U.S.A.

Website address: www.lernerbooks.com

Library of Congress Cataloging-in-Publication Data

Shaw, Murray.
    Sherlock Holmes and the Boscombe Valley mystery / based on the stories
of Sir Arthur Conan Doyle ; adapted by Murray Shaw and M.J. Cosson ;
illustrated by Sophie Rohrbach and J.T. Morrow.
        p.   cm. — (On the case with Holmes and Watson ; #10)
    Summary: Retold in graphic novel form, Sherlock Holmes attempts
to solve the murder of a Herefordshire landowner, whose estranged son
has been accused of the crime. Includes a section explaining Holmes's
reasoning and the clues he used to solve the mystery.
    ISBN: 978-0-7613-7089-5 (lib. bdg. : alk. paper)
    I. Graphic novels. (I. Graphic novels. 2. Doyle, Arthur Conan, Sir,
1859–1930. Boscombe Valley mystery—Adaptations. 3. Mystery and detective
stories.) I. Cosson, M. J. II. Rohrbach, Sophie, ill. III. Morrow, J. T., ill.
IV. Doyle, Arthur Conan, Sir, 1859–1930. Boscombe Valley mystery. V. Title.
VI. Title: Boscombe Valley mystery.
    PZ7.7.S46Sib 2012
    741.5'973—dc22   2010040725

Manufactured in the United States of America
1—BC—7/15/11

The Story of
SHERLOCK HOLMES
the Famous Detective

Sherlock Holmes and his helpful friend Dr. John Watson are fictional characters created by British writer Sir Arthur Conan Doyle. Doyle published his first novel about the pair, *A Study in Scarlet*, in 1887, and it became very successful. Doyle went on to write fifty-six short stories, as well as three more novels about Holmes's adventures—*The Sign of Four* (1890), *The Hound of the Baskervilles* (1902), and *The Valley of Fear* (1915).

Sherlock Holmes and Dr. Watson have become some of the most famous book characters of all time. Holmes spent most of his time solving mysteries, but he also had a wide array of hobbies, such as playing the violin, boxing, and sword fighting. Watson, a retired army doctor, met Holmes through a mutual friend when Holmes was looking for a roommate. Watson lived with Holmes for several years at 221B Baker Street before marrying and moving out. However, after his marriage, Watson continued to assist Holmes with his cases.

The original versions of the Sherlock Holmes stories are still printed, and many have been made into movies and television shows. Readers continue to be impressed by Holmes's detective methods of observation and scientific reason.

Sherlock Holmes   Dr. Watson

James McCarthy

Mrs. Watson

Lodgekeeper Moran   Mrs. Moran

John Turner

Alice Turner

Charles McCarthy

Maid

William Crowder

Patricia Moran

Inspector Lestrade

From the Desk of
John H. Watson, M.D.

My name is Dr. John H. Watson. For several years, I have been assisting my friend, Sherlock Holmes, in solving mysteries throughout the bustling city of London and beyond. Holmes is a peculiar man—always questioning and reasoning his way through various problems. But when I first met him in 1878, I was immediately intrigued by his oddities.

Holmes has always been more daring than I, and his logical deduction never ceases to amaze me. I have begun writing down all of the adventures I have with Holmes. This is one of those stories.

Sincerely,

Dr. Watson

My army experience in Afghanistan had taught me to pack quickly and lightly. So I was soon in a cab, rattling away to Paddington Station. Holmes was awaiting me there, pacing up and down the platform.

NOW FOR THE EVENT. LAST MONDAY MORNING, JUNE 3, CHARLES MCCARTHY TOLD HIS SERVANT THAT HE HAD AN APPOINTMENT TO KEEP AT THREE O'CLOCK.

AT CLOSE TO THREE, MCCARTHY WALKED DOWN TO THE BOSCOMBE POOL. THIS IS A SMALL POND THAT IS HALFWAY BETWEEN HATHERLEY FARM AND THE TURNER ESTATE.

MCCARTHY NEVER CAME BACK FROM THIS APPOINTMENT *ALIVE.*

WILLIAM CROWDER, THE GAMEKEEPER FOR TURNER'S PROPERTIES, SAW MCCARTHY ON HIS WAY TO THE POOL. MCCARTHY WAS ALONE.

WITHIN A FEW MINUTES, CROWDER SAW MCCARTHY'S SON, JAMES. THE YOUNG MAN HAD A GUN UNDER HIS ARM AND WAS GOING THE SAME WAY. AT THE TIME, CROWDER THOUGHT JAMES WAS FOLLOWING HIS FATHER.

THE GIRL HAD HARDLY FINISHED DESCRIBING THE EVENT WHEN JAMES MCCARTHY CAME RUNNING UP TO THE LODGE. HE WAS EXTREMELY UPSET AND HAD NEITHER HIS GUN NOR HIS HAT. FRESH BLOOD STAINED HIS RIGHT HAND AND SLEEVE.

HELP! PLEASE HELP! MY FATHER IS DEAD!

JAMES BEGGED THE LODGEKEEPER TO COME WITH HIM TO WHERE HIS FATHER LAY.

THE LODGEKEEPER FOUND THE BODY NEXT TO THE POOL. THE HEAD HAD BEEN STRUCK BY A BLUNT WEAPON. THE END OF THE SON'S RIFLE COULD HAVE MADE THE WOUND, BUT IT HAD NO BLOOD ON IT. THE GUN WAS FOUND IN THE GRASS ONLY A FEW PACES FROM THE BODY.

JAMES MCCARTHY WAS LATER ARRESTED AND CHARGED WITH THE MURDER OF HIS FATHER.

I SEE. I COULD HARDLY IMAGINE A MORE HOPELESS CASE FOR THE BOY. ALL THE CIRCUMSTANCES POINT TO HIM.

TRUE, BUT EVIDENCE OF THIS TYPE CAN BE TRICKY. IF ONE APPROACHES THE EVIDENCE FROM A DIFFERENT DIRECTION, IT SUDDENLY POINTS TO THE OPPOSITE CONCLUSION.

FOR EXAMPLE, YOUNG JAMES DID NOT SEEM THE LEAST BIT SURPRISED TO BE ARRESTED.

AH, WELL, THIS IS CERTAINLY NO MORE THAN I DESERVE.

THERE WE HAVE A CONFESSION! THAT ALONE SHOULD PROVE HIS GUILT, SHOULD IT NOT?

NOT AT ALL, WATSON. IMMEDIATELY AFTER SAYING THESE THINGS, MCCARTHY DECLARED HIS INNOCENCE.

HE WOULD HAVE TO HAVE BEEN A FOOL, INDEED, NOT TO HAVE SEEN THE CASE AGAINST HIM.

IF HE HAD ACTED SURPRISED OR OUTRAGED, I WOULD HAVE TRUSTED HIM LESS. BUT MCCARTHY COVERED UP NOTHING.

HE SEEMED TO FEEL A GREAT GUILT FOR HAVING ARGUED WITH HIS FATHER. THESE ACTIONS SEEM TO ME TO BE SIGNS OF AN INNOCENT MIND.

15

MAYBE SO, HOLMES, BUT MANY MEN HAVE BEEN HANGED ON FAR LESS EVIDENCE.

YES, AND MANY MEN HAVE BEEN WRONGFULLY HANGED.

DOES MCCARTHY'S OWN STORY SHED ANY HOPE ON HIS CASE?

I'M AFRAID IT IS NOT VERY ENCOURAGING, WATSON. TAKE A LOOK FOR YOURSELF.

THE LOCAL PAPER HAD DEVOTED A LONG SECTION TO THE INITIAL INVESTIGATION.

HEREFORDSHIRE HERALD

THE SECTION EXPLAINED HOW THE EXAMINER HAD QUESTIONED JAMES MCCARTHY.

TELL US WHAT YOU KNOW OF THIS TRAGEDY.

I HAD BEEN AWAY IN BRISTOL. WHEN I RETURNED, I LEARNED THAT MY FATHER HAD GONE TO ROSS, THE NEAREST MARKET TOWN TO HATHERLEY.

SOME TIME LATER, I GLANCED OUT THE WINDOW AND SAW HIS CARRIAGE ARRIVE. HE GOT OUT AND BEGAN WALKING AWAY FROM THE HOUSE.

I WAS NOT MORE THAN A 150 YARDS AWAY WHEN I HEARD A HIDEOUS CRY OF PAIN AND CAME RUNNING BACK. MY FATHER WAS ON THE GROUND, BLEEDING TERRIBLY. I DROPPED MY GUN AND PICKED HIM UP IN MY ARMS. HE SOON DIED.

I HELD HIM FOR A FEW MINUTES AND THEN RAN TO THE LODGEKEEPER'S FOR HELP. I DON'T KNOW HOW HE CAME TO BE WOUNDED. MR. CROWDER WAS THE ONLY PERSON I HAD SEEN IN THE AREA.

WHY DID YOU AND YOUR FATHER QUARREL?

I WOULD PREFER NOT TO ANSWER THAT. IT HAD NOTHING TO DO WITH WHAT HAPPENED.

IF YOUR FATHER DID NOT KNOW YOU WERE NEAR, WHY SHOULD HE YELL "COOEE"?

I DO NOT KNOW.

19

23

After they left, I tried to interest myself in a novel. But the plot seemed flat compared to the real-life story of James McCarthy. So I picked up the local paper Holmes had left. It gave a description of the injury found on McCarthy's head.

YOU DO HAVE DIFFICULTY TACKLING THE FACTS.

WELL, I CAN SEE ONE FACT CLEARLY ENOUGH. THE BOY KILLED HIS FATHER. ALL THE REST IS NONSENSE.

MAYBE SO, BUT THE CASE ISN'T CLOSED YET!

NOW IF I'M NOT MISTAKEN, THAT'S HATHERLEY FARM ON OUR LEFT.

A MAID ANSWERED THE DOOR.

AT HOLMES'S REQUEST, SHE BROUGHT HIM THE BOOTS OF HER DEAD MASTER, AS WELL AS THOSE OF HIS SON.

HOLMES MEASURED EACH BOOT FROM SOME SEVEN OR EIGHT POINTS.

Back and forth, Holmes worked, eventually stopping at the base of a tree some yards from the crime scene. In the moss around the roots, he discovered the butt of a small cigar and ashes. He passed them to me for inspection. The unsmoked end of the cigar had been bluntly cut and had not been bitten. Holmes moved on to examine a large, jagged stone. He had found it lying on the grass near one of the tree roots.

The inspector snickered in disbelief but said nothing more. Holmes left us in the carriage and made a quick detour on foot to the lodgekeeper's house to leave a message.

When Holmes returned, Lestrade drove us back to the inn. Holmes seemed in quite a jovial mood.

36

I MEANT HIS BOY NO HARM. I WOULD HAVE COME FORWARD IF THE COURT RULED AGAINST HIM. I JUST WANTED TO PROTECT MY DAUGHTER.

IT MAY NOT COME TO THAT. BUT YOU MUST TELL ME THE TRUTH, OR I MAY NOT BE ABLE TO HELP YOU.

MR. HOLMES, I AM DYING.

I HAVE HAD DIABETES FOR YEARS. I MAY NOT LIVE OUT THE MONTH. I WOULD LIKE TO DIE UNDER MY OWN ROOF. SO I WILL TELL YOU EVERYTHING.

MCCARTHY WAS A DEVIL OF A MAN, I TELL YOU. FOR TWENTY YEARS, HIS GRIP HAS BEEN UPON ME. IT ALL BEGAN BACK IN THE EARLY SIXTIES AT THE DIGGINGS IN AUSTRALIA.

41

WHEN I WENT DOWN TO MEET MCCARTHY, I SAW HIM ARGUING WITH HIS SON. SO I HID BEHIND A LARGE TREE AND SMOKED MY CIGAR WHILE I WAITED.

WHAT THAT BEAST SAID TO HIS SON MADE MY BLOOD BOIL! I THINK I WENT A BIT MAD.

AS SOON AS HIS SON LEFT, I PICKED UP A LARGE STONE, SNEAKED UP ON MCCARTHY, AND HIT HIM WITH ALL MY STRENGTH.

Old John Turner lived only a few months after we spoke to him. Because of objections raised by Holmes, the courts found James McCarthy to be innocent. No one else was ever accused of the murder. We have heard recently that young McCarthy may soon wed Alice Turner. It is hoped that they will live quite happily. May they never know the black cloud that rests upon their past.

The Boscombe Valley Mystery:
How Did Holmes Solve It?

How did Holmes deduce that there was more than one suspect?

Since Charles McCarthy had gone to the Boscombe Pool to meet someone, there were automatically two suspects for the murder: James McCarthy and the person McCarthy had gone to meet. The gamekeeper, Mr. Crowder, also was a suspect, since he had been nearby at the time of the murder.

What clue initially led Holmes to consider Turner as a suspect?

According to James McCarthy, his father had called out the Australian greeting "cooee." Since this signal was not meant for James, Charles could have been waiting to meet someone else from Australia. Therefore, Holmes paid close attention to all the facts about McCarthy's Australian friend—John Turner.

How did McCarthy's mumbling about "a rat" help lead Holmes to the culprit?

The maid told Holmes the place in Australia where Turner and McCarthy had met was called Ballarat. The ending could sound like "a rat." The maid had not heard of any recent letters or visits to Mr. McCarthy from Australians. So, Turner immediately became the prime suspect.

What other clue led Holmes to consider Turner as a suspect?

Holmes also figured there must be some bad feelings between John Turner and Charles McCarthy, since Turner did not want his daughter to marry McCarthy's son. This was another strike against Turner.

How did Holmes's examination of the murder scene lead him to Turner?

By the long lengths between the square-toed footprints, Holmes could see that the murderer was a tall man. The footprints also showed that the man leaned heavily on one foot, so Holmes knew that he limped. The fact that McCarthy had been hit on the left side of his head from behind made it likely that the murderer was left-handed. And finally, by studying the ashes and cigar left at the scene, Holmes could even describe the criminal's smoking habits. All that was left was to find the man who fit this description.

How could Holmes be so certain that he had the right man?

Holmes sent Turner a message, and the man came. Turner fit all the details of the murderer's description. Holmes had no doubt that he had found the right man.

Further Reading and Websites

Baker Street Journal
http://www.bakerstreetjournal.com

Banting, Erinn. *Australia: The People.* New York: Crabtree, 2003.

Carey, Benedict. *The Unknowns.* New York: Amulet Books, 2009.

Dowd, Siobhan. *The London Eye Mystery.* New York: Random House, 2009.

Gregory, Kristiana. *The Clue at the Bottom of the Lake.* New York: Scholastic, 2008.

Marsh, Carole. *The Mystery of the Great Barrier Reef: Sydney, Australia.* New York: Gallopade International, 2006.

McCollum, Sean. *Australia.* Minneapolis: Lerner Publications Company, 2008.

Sherlock Holmes Museum
http://www.sherlock-holmes.co.uk

Sir Arthur Conan Doyle Society
http://www.ash-tree.bc.ca/acdsocy.html

Townsend, John. *Forensic Evidence: Prints.* New York: Crabtree Publishing, 2008.

221 Baker Street
http://221bakerstreet.org

About the Author

Sir Arthur Conan Doyle was born on May 22, 1859. He became a doctor in 1882. When this career did not prove successful, Doyle started writing stories. In addition to the popular Sherlock Holmes short stories and novels, Doyle also wrote historical novels, romances, and plays.

About the Adapters

Murray Shaw's lifelong passion for Sherlock Holmes began when he was a child. He was the author of the Match Wits with Sherlock Holmes series published in the 1990s. For decades, he was a popular speaker in public schools and libraries on the adventures of Holmes and Watson.

M. J. Cosson is the author of more than fifty books, both fiction and nonfiction, for children and young adults. She has long been a fan of mysteries and especially of the great detective, Sherlock Holmes. In fact, she has participated in the production of several Sherlock Holmes plays. A native of Iowa, Cosson lives in the Texas Hill Country with her husband, dogs, and cat.

About the Illustrators

Sophie Rohrbach began her career after graduating in display design at the Chambre des Commerce in France. She went on to design displays in many top department stores including Galerias Lafayette. She also studied illustration at Emile Cohl school in Lyon, France, where she now lives with her daughter. Rohrbach has illustrated many children's books. She is passionate about the colors and patterns that she uses in her illustrations.

JT Morrow has worked as a freelance illustrator for over twenty years and has won several awards. He specializes in doing parodies and imitations of the Old and Modern Masters—everyone from da Vinci to Picasso. JT also exhibits his paintings at galleries near his home. He lives just south of San Francisco with his wife and daughter.